D1459126

PETER BOWMAN

TINY TED

RED FOX

TINY TED
A RED FOX BOOK 978 1 862 30692 9

First published in Great Britain by Hutchinson,
an imprint of Random House Children's Books
A Random House Group Company

Hutchinson edition published 1994
Red Fox edition published 1997
This Red Fox edition published 2008

1 3 5 7 9 10 8 6 4 2

Red Fox books are published by Random House Children's Books,
61–63 Uxbridge Road, London W5 5SA

www.kidsatrandomhouse.co.uk
www.rbooks.co.uk

Addresses for companies within The Random House Group Limited can
be found at: www.randomhouse.co.uk/offices.htm

THE RANDOM HOUSE GROUP Limited Reg. No. 954009

A CIP catalogue record for this book is available from the British Library.

Printed in China

This edition is part of a box set and cannot be sold or returned separately.

From the case on the wall came a big sigh.

'I'm fed up with
being on the shelf,'
said Tiny Ted.

'No one ever
talks to me...'

'...and just look at the
dust and cobwebs!'

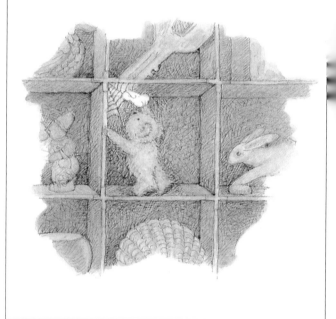

'I wonder
what the
world is like
down there...'

'Atishoo!'

'Phew!
A nice
soft
landing.'

'Oh no!
It's not a mat.
It's a cat!'

'Phew, that was close.
I think I'll hide
behind these logs.'

'Oh, what lovely colours!'

'Hey! It's that cat again.'

'Help!'

'It's chasing me!'

'Goodness! It's not very safe down here.'

'I think I'll just
hide in this box
until the coast
is clear.'

'Oh no! It's somebody's house.'

BOING!

'Where am I now? Eeeek, MONSTERS!'

'I've had enough.
Will someone please
take me home?'

'Just a little bit higher...'

'...Whoops!
Not high
enough.'

'Oh, well, this is cosy.
Maybe I'll have a little nap.'

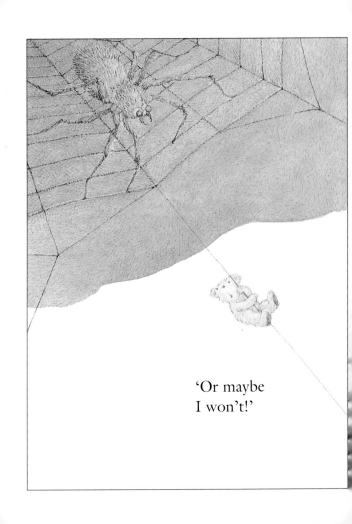

'Or maybe
I won't!'

'Hello, I'm Tiny Ted.
I'd love to dance.'

'But I've gone all dizzy.'

'I think I'm better on the ground.
That looks tasty.'

'Ouch! My paws.'

'Whoops. Pardon me.
It's just that I'm lost
and alone, and very,
very small.'

'Oh, you are kind,'
said Tiny Ted.
'Safe at last!'
And he was.